A
WINTER
KILL

A WINTER KILL

VICKI DELANY

RAVEN BOOKS
an imprint of
ORCA BOOK PUBLISHERS

Library and Archives Canada Cataloguing in Publication

Delany, Vicki, 1951-
A winter kill / Vicki Delany.
(Rapid reads)

Issued also in electronic formats.
ISBN 978-1-55469-956-8

I. Title. II. Series: Rapid reads.
PS8557.E4239W56 2012   C813'.6   C2011-907568-7

First published in the United States, 2012
Library of Congress Control Number: 2011942470

Summary: When rookie police constable Nicole Patterson discovers
a body on the edge of town, she's drawn into a murder investigation
that's well beyond her experience and expertise. (RL 2.8)

*Orca Book Publishers is dedicated to preserving the environment and has
printed this book on paper certified by the Forest Stewardship Council®.*

Orca Book Publishers gratefully acknowledges the support for
its publishing programs provided by the following agencies:
the Government of Canada through the Canada Book Fund and the
Canada Council for the Arts, and the Province of British Columbia
through the BC Arts Council and the Book Publishing Tax Credit.

Design by Teresa Bubela
Cover photography by Getty Images

ORCA BOOK PUBLISHERS
PO Box 5626, Stn. B
Victoria, BC Canada
V8R 6S4

ORCA BOOK PUBLISHERS
PO Box 468
Custer, WA USA
98240-0468

www.orcabook.com
Printed and bound in Canada.

15 14 13 12 • 4 3 2 1

For my mother, a teacher

CHAPTER ONE

Sometimes you can just tell.
　　When they're dead.

They don't have to even look dead.
Not really. More like they're sleeping.

There's something different about
a dead body.

You can always tell.

I haven't seen many dead bodies.
Not yet. I've only been a cop for six months.

I took a deep breath and swung the beam
of my flashlight around the field. I touched
the radio at my shoulder with one hand
and the Sig Sauer at my hip with the other.

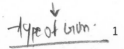 type of gun.

Trying to steady my nerves. The sky above was pitch black, and it was very cold.

A plastic bag that had blown up against the rusty wire fence moved. My heart jumped into my throat. It was only a cat. Yellow eyes glared at me. It hissed once and darted off. Its tail swayed in the still air and then it was gone.

All was quiet. A single car drove down the road. It did not stop. When I thought I could breathe properly again, I spoke into the radio. "Dispatch. Three-oh. One-oh-two."

"Go ahead, one-oh-two."

"I'm on Kingsley Road, not far from County Road Twenty-two. Near the airfield. VSA. I need an ambulance and backup."

VSA, the dispatcher knew, means vital signs absent. A dead body in other words.

This road was well out of town. The moon and the distant lights of Picton

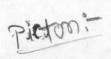

were hidden by thick clouds. The long rows of boarded-up buildings on the abandoned World War II airfield were dark. Amber and white security lights did little to break the night. The flashing red and blue of my patrol car reflected off the snow.

I shifted my feet. Snow crunched beneath my boots. I dropped to a squat beside the body. It was a woman. Her long pink scarf was wrapped tightly around her neck. Too tight to let air pass. I ran the beam of my flashlight across her face. Her eyes bulged. Her mouth hung open and a swollen pink tongue stuck out. A silver ball was pierced through the middle. She had piercings running up her right ear and in one eyebrow. I pulled off my gloves and held my fingers to the side of her neck. Cold and still.

She was dressed in jeans and scruffy running shoes and a bright blue jacket. Threads escaped from an old tear in the jacket sleeve. Her hands were bare even though the temperature was well below freezing. She must have been very cold. Before she died.

Her hands were the color of skim milk, white touched with blue. Her jeans were unzipped and pulled down past her hips. I could see the lacy trim of a pink thong. But the jeans were still on, the girl's legs together. Had this been an attempted rape? If so, it had not gone very far.

Had something, or someone, scared him away?

It wasn't me. This girl had been dead for more than a few minutes.

I looked into her face and saw something familiar. Her skin was clean of makeup and her blond hair shone in the beam of my flashlight.

She was local. I'd seen her around. I was pretty sure she went to Prince Edward District High School.

At the welcome sound of sirens I let out a breath I hadn't known I was holding in. Coming my way. Police car first, then an ambulance. I wanted to lower the girl's lids over her bulging eyes, but knew not to disturb the scene. I pushed myself to my feet and lifted my flashlight. I shone the beam of light across the field to the road, letting them know where I was.

The snow was very deep. It was all churned up around here, but I couldn't see any boot tracks. The body was a couple of yards from the road. It looked as if a vehicle had pulled in. She'd been dragged out of a car and dumped. Then whoever had done it had brushed away his tracks and driven off.

The light shone on something half buried in the snow. A piece of blue glass. I reached out my hand to pick it up, before remembering where I was.

And who I was.

A probationary cop with the Ontario Provincial Police in Prince Edward County, Ontario.

My name is Nicole Patterson. I'm twenty-four years old. I've been with the OPP for six months. This was a peaceful, mostly rural community. Lots of farms. Wineries and art galleries. Bed-and-breakfasts and tourist rentals close to the long sandy beaches of Sandbanks Provincial Park. Nice big homes for retired baby boomers from Toronto. Pretty scenery, proud people. Not much in the way of crime.

Before that night I'd seen two dead bodies. An old man who died alone a week before his neighbor began to wonder what the smell was. And a sixteen-year-old boy with a brand-new driver's license who thought he was too cool to wear his seat belt. He skidded on a patch of black ice and went into a hydro pole straight on.

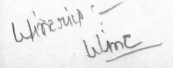

That was not cool.

The siren came closer and the field flooded with light.

"What you got, Patterson?" a man's deep voice asked.

Sergeant Paul Malan, the detachment's lead detective, was walking toward me. He was tall and thin, a runner's body. His hair was cut short and his silver mustache was neatly trimmed. Behind him came the smaller frame of Constable Larry Johnstone.

I swung my flashlight to the ground. The young woman stared up at us through empty eyes. She was partially hidden behind a clump of bushes. I wouldn't have seen her except that her legs were sticking out. The headlights of my cruiser had caught the white running shoes.

The paramedics stood back, watching. They had their stretcher out, piled with equipment bags. Malan made no move to invite them to move in.

There was no hurry.

"Look at that," I said, pointing to the blue glass.

Malan crouched down and studied the object. Johnstone looked over his shoulder. The sergeant pulled a pen out of his pocket and slowly scooped the blue stone out of the snow. It was a ring. A large blue piece of glass set in a silver band. It didn't look as if it cost very much.

Malan pulled a plastic bag out of his pocket and dropped the ring in.

"Know her?" he asked me.

"She goes to Prince Edward District High."

"Name?"

I shrugged. "Don't know it."

"Okay. Let's seal this area off. Johnstone, park your vehicle up the road a couple hundred yards. Patterson, watch the intersection. No one in or out other than police. Log everyone who comes by."

"Got it," Larry Johnstone grunted. He was also a new officer. He'd been on the force for about two years. I took one last look at the young woman on the ground. Her blond hair was long and straight. It shone in the headlights from the ambulance. She had been pretty, I remembered.

She was pretty no more.

Log :→ Record - -

Crouched down:→ band

hiA knee .

CHAPTER TWO

"Patterson, you're with me."

"Yes, sir. Uh, where are we going?"

Sergeant Malan had walked through the snow to the road where I'd spent the past few hours keeping the curious away. "The girl has ID in her pocket. School card. I'm going to her house and need a ride. You can drive me."

"Yes, sir," I said. The forensic officers had arrived before the sun began to rise. Guys in white suits sifting through the snow and debris of the field. Looking for clues. For evidence. The paramedics had been allowed to take the body away. Yellow crime-scene tape protected the area. A few people had gathered to watch. They stood beside their cars on the opposite side of County Road 22. They were dressed in winter coats, scarves and heavy gloves. We got into my cruiser. Malan fastened his seat belt.

"This won't be easy," he said. "Never is."

"Yes, sir."

She'd lived in a run-down part of town, at the bottom of the hill where the abandoned airfield was. The houses were old. Some of them were neat and tidy, but many were badly looked after. Thin, scruffy trees lined the street. Snow was piled in dirty banks. All the lights were off. It was very quiet.

The driveway hadn't been shoveled. I parked in the street. "I've been here before," I said.

"We've all been to this house before," Malan said. "Noise complaints, drunk and disorderly, fights. One time Grey couldn't be bothered to go inside to take a leak. He pissed on his neighbor's front lawn. Won't make it any easier to tell him his daughter's dead though." We got out of the car. As we walked up the cracked and broken cement steps, a dog started to bark.

A piece of masking tape was stuck over the doorbell. Malan knocked. I shifted in my boots. It was very cold. Our breath formed little puffs in the air.

Malan knocked again. And again. Louder each time. Then a light came on at the back of the house. The barking dog got closer.

The front door opened a crack. "What the fuck do you want?" a man said. His hair was thin and unwashed. His eyes were small and very red. He blinked away sleep. He smelled of unbrushed teeth and stale beer.

"Mr. Grey," Malan said. "May we come in?"

"Not without a warrant, you can't."

"You're not in any trouble. Do you have a daughter by the name of Maureen?"

"What the fuck's she done now?"

"Mr. Grey, is Maureen at home?"

"What business is that of yours?"

"What is it?" asked another voice from inside the house. It was a woman's voice, low and frightened.

"Mrs. Grey, I'm sorry to disturb you, but I'm afraid I have some very bad news. It would be better if we discussed this inside."

For the first time, Grey looked at me. I tried to keep my face still. He looked me up and down, and I felt very uncomfortable.

"Let the officers in," the woman said. "If they have news about Maureen."

Grey hesitated, and then he shrugged and opened the door.

The dog lunged for us. Grey laughed as I jumped backward with a frightened cry.

It was a big dog. Traces of German shepherd. Half its right ear was missing and its teeth were yellow. But the animal didn't get near me. Mrs. Grey was holding tightly to its leash.

"Put the dog in another room, please," Malan said.

The woman looked at her husband. He shrugged, and she dragged the snarling animal away.

Sergeant Malan and I stepped into the house. The living-room furniture was shabby, but no dust was on it. Aside from many ornaments, the room was uncluttered, but it smelled of cigarette smoke and cooking grease. Mrs. Grey came back. She twisted her hands in her faded blue nightgown.

"You have a daughter named Maureen?" Malan asked. His voice was soft and kind.

The Greys nodded.

"Is Maureen at home?"

"Nah," Grey said. "She moved out a while ago."

His wife's eyes were wide with fear. "Is she in some sort of trouble? Maureen left home a few weeks ago. A temporary move. She's been having problems at school. She needed a break. She's staying with a friend."

"Do you have the friend's address?"

"No."

"The name of this friend?"

She shook her head.

Maureen Grey had left home and her parents didn't know where she'd gone. I'd call that running away, not taking a break. But I wasn't here to express my opinion.

Malan reached into his pocket. Slowly he pulled out the student card from PE District High. I caught a glimpse of the picture. A blond girl, smiling broadly.

"Is this your daughter?" he asked Mrs. Grey. She reached out and took the card. Her hand was shaking.

"Yes." Her voice was so soft it was hard to hear. "It's Maureen. It's my daughter."

"I'm sorry to have to tell you this," Malan said. "We found a body, a young girl, in the snow outside of town. She had this on her."

Mrs. Grey let out a moan. She shook her head. "No, that can't be right. Some other girl must have been carrying her school card. You've made a mistake."

Her husband made no move to comfort her. "Where is she?" he asked Malan.

"She's been taken to the hospital. If you'll get dressed, we'll take you to see her. We'll need you to make a positive identification."

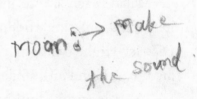

moan → make the sound

CHAPTER THREE

A couple of days later I ran into Sergeant Malan in the lunchroom at the station. I was back on day shift, and as usual things were pretty quiet in the County in winter. He came in as I was filling the kettle to make a cup of tea to take on the road. He dug into the fridge for a plastic container. He sat at the big table in the center of the room and took out his sandwich. It looked good. Thickly sliced roast beef and Swiss cheese on whole-wheat bread. Bright yellow mustard leaked from the sides.

"Nicole," he said. "You're the one who found her, right? You'll be interested in this. I'm just back from the Maureen Grey autopsy."

"What'd they find?" I asked. I was interested. Right now I'm just a probationary constable, still pretty wet behind the ears and nervous whenever I get a call. But one day I might like to be a detective. "I figured it looked pretty obvious. She was strangled by that scarf."

"That was the cause of death, yes. She'd been dead for two or three hours when you found her. There were no defensive wounds. No marks on her arms or hands to show she tried to fight off her attacker. Her fingernails were torn where she tried to get a grip on the scarf. Plenty of fibers from the scarf under her nails. A big bruise on her rear end where the attacker pressed his knee against her to hold her steady while he—or she—choked her."

"What does that mean?"

"She was taken by surprise. Either her attacker snuck up on her or she didn't expect him to attack her. It would have been over very fast."

"I can't see that anyone could have surprised someone out there. In a field in the middle of the night?"

"I agree. Highly unlikely she would have gone there alone. And not without gloves. There were none in her pockets, and we couldn't find any nearby. Almost certainly she arrived in a car. And the driver of the car either killed her there or dumped the body. And drove off."

"Can you tell anything from the bruise? About the size or height of the attacker?"

He smiled at me. "Good question, Constable." I was childishly pleased at the praise. The other night was the first time I'd even spoken to the detective sergeant.

He didn't have much to do with a mere probationary constable.

"Yes, the assailant was around the same height as the girl, perhaps a bit more. She was very tall at five foot ten, so that includes a lot of men. Also any woman who might be shorter but was wearing boots with high heels."

"So the autopsy didn't tell you much?"

"Actually, Nicole, it told me a lot. Maureen Grey was four months pregnant."

"Wow. I wonder if that's important."

"If you want hot water, you'd better get it," he said. "The kettle stopped boiling a long time ago."

I felt blood rush into my face. I blush very easily, and that's a bad thing for a police officer. I busied myself with a tea bag, milk and sugar.

"It might explain why she wasn't living at her parents' house," Malan said. "Her father has a bad temper and is quick with his fists. He might not have taken the news that he was about to become a grandfather very well."

"Maybe he killed her when he found out?"

"It's possible. Anything's possible. I can't really see Grey sneaking up behind his daughter and strangling her. He's more a fist to the mouth sort of guy. Plus, he doesn't own a vehicle. His truck was repossessed about a month ago. But he has plenty of friends who'd lend him their car, no questions asked. There's no telling what a man like that is capable of. I can't help but think the pregnancy might have had something to do with her death."

"Her clothes were disturbed. Was she...?"

"Raped? Molested? No. Either pulling down her pants was an attempt to make us think it was a rape or the guy was scared away."

"But she was dead already? You said it was quick."

The sergeant gave me a long look. He was in his forties. He had transferred to the OPP about a year ago from the Toronto Police Service. Station gossip said he wanted a quieter life and more family time. I knew that he was married and had two young kids, a boy and a girl. A picture of the smiling family sat on his desk. His wife was pretty and stylish, and the children cute and well-scrubbed.

"Sometimes," he said, "the rapist doesn't want to be bothered struggling with a victim."

For a moment I wasn't quite sure what he was saying. Then I understood and my blood ran cold. "You mean," I said, "they like the women dead."

He nodded. "Sometimes. In this case it might have been rough sex gone badly wrong. Guy sees she's dead. He panics, dumps her and drives away. But that's unlikely if she was standing when he attacked her. The autopsy found no signs of recent intercourse."

"Do you have any suspects?"

He shook his head. "Other than Pete Grey? No one obvious. I've interviewed her teachers and the kids at her school. No one mentioned her being pregnant. Now I'll have to go back and ask the people she seemed close to if she'd told anyone about it. We can't find her cell phone. Everyone at the school said she had one. They all do these days, don't they? It would help, a lot, if we could see who'd called her the night she died. Almost certainly her killer dumped it somewhere."

The radio on my shoulder crackled. It was dispatch. Two boys had grabbed a stack of chocolate bars off the rack at a convenience store and bolted for it.

"Gotta go," I said.

He lifted a hand in farewell and bit into his sandwich.

I never did get that cup of tea.

CHAPTER FOUR

Unlike Sergeant Malan, I'm a County girl. Born and bred. I went away to university and spent four years in Toronto. I hated the big city—the noise, the crowds, the pollution. But there aren't many good jobs in the country these days. I was lucky to get on with the OPP and be able to come back to Prince Edward County. Where I belong. Someday I might have to think about going back to the city. If I want to get a range of solid police experience and climb the ladder. But for now I'm content to be here.

I had an apartment in town, but my parents, Janet and Roy, still lived on the farm outside of Milford where I grew up. Mom and Dad hoped I'd take over the farm some day. I love the country life, but being a farmer just never appealed to me. Too much hard work, maybe. My younger sister, Sandy, was going to university in Ottawa next fall. My parents were hoping she'd come back to the farm. Sandy wants to be a doctor.

My mom volunteered twice a week at the Prince Edward County Youth Center. It's a drop-in place. Teenagers can hang out, play some games, use the computers to do homework in a quiet setting. Maybe get advice on career and life choices. The center's important to Mom. She was working hard to get funding to open a small café. It would serve hot food and drinks and give the kids some work experience.

I'd quickly found the boys who'd stolen the chocolate bars. They were standing on the next street over, stuffing chocolate into their mouths. Ten years old.

When my shift ended, I changed out of my uniform and drove to the youth center. Maureen Grey might have gone there sometimes. Maybe Mom knew her.

She did.

"Such a tragedy," Mom said after we'd said hi. "It's upset the students a lot. We got a counselor to come in and help some of the kids here deal with it. I think that's helped."

We were in the office. It was a cramped room with a badly stuffed couch and a battered desk. A cork notice board on the wall was covered with scraps of paper. The glass wall of the office looked out over the reading room. A couple of teenagers slouched over a table, glancing at textbooks. They were waiting for their turn on one of the two computers. The computers were good up-to-date ones. They'd been donated by a local company.

Slouched :27 hanging

"Can you tell me anything about Maureen?" I asked my mother.

"Like what?"

"Did Sergeant Malan or Detective Roberts come here to ask about her?"

"I don't think so."

"Did you know her well, Mom?"

"Not really. Maureen was a nice girl. Quiet. Hardworking. They don't have a computer in her home, so she came here to use ours. I liked her. I felt sorry for her. With those no-good parents and..."

"And what?"

"I'd rather not say."

"Mom, if you know something you have to tell me. We don't have any leads. You might be able to help."

"I don't like to gossip."

"It's not gossip if you tell a police officer." I didn't mention that I'm not a detective. No one had told me to get involved. But I know people in small towns in a way that

Sergeant Malan wouldn't. I'd poke around a bit. See if I could find anything important.

"I'm sorry to say." My mom began to talk very slowly. As if the words tasted bad in her mouth. "Maureen had a reputation."

"What sort of a reputation?"

"She was...well, she dated a lot of the boys at school."

"What's wrong with that?" I asked. "If she was popular?"

Mom was looking at me very strangely.

"Oh," I said. "You don't mean dating. You mean she screwed around."

Mom nodded. "That's the reputation she had. I never saw her with more than the occasional boy. But it does often happen in families such as hers. A girl gets no love from her father so she looks for it somewhere else."

"Like with boys at school?"

"That's right. Poor Maureen. She didn't have many girlfriends. I heard the other girls talking about her sometimes. Teenage girls can be pretty mean. When they get an idea in their minds, and someone to bully, stories can get...exaggerated."

I had been a teenager not long ago. I knew Mom was right.

"Boys did seem to pay attention to her. I'd heard that a couple of boys had slept with her. And then they dumped her and called her names to their buddies. At least that's what people say. It might or might not be true." Mom has a cheerful face with round chubby cheeks and a big smile. Now she looked like an unhappy Mrs. Santa Claus.

"Any boy in particular?" I asked.

"I don't know who she was dating lately. She wasn't coming into the center as much in the last few weeks as she used to. Do you think that's important?"

"I don't know. I'm going to tell you something you cannot tell anyone else. Okay?"

"I don't gossip," my mother said.

No one else was in the office, but I leaned over anyway. "She was four months pregnant."

Mom didn't look surprised.

"You knew?" I said.

"I guessed. She normally dressed like teenagers do these days. Tight T-shirts. Short skirts. Clinging jeans. Then she started wearing loose sweaters and baggy pants. I came into the bathroom one day right after her. She'd been throwing up. I could smell it."

I thought for a while. "Any talk," I said, "about her having relationships with adults? Teachers maybe?"

"Not that I ever heard."

"Thanks for your help, Mom."

"You're coming for dinner on Sunday."

Oh God "Gee, I don't know if..."

"You're coming for dinner on Sunday," my mother said.

leaned — 31

CHAPTER FIVE

Two girls were standing on the steps outside the youth center, smoking. One of them dropped her cigarette to the snowy sidewalk. She ground it under her foot and went back inside. The second girl was staring at me. I gave her a smile.

"You're Mrs. Patterson's daughter, right?" she said. She flicked her cigarette butt onto the ground.

"Yes. I'm Nicole."

She shifted from one foot to another. She wore a long black wool coat with shiny gold buttons and a thick red scarf.

Her boots were leather. She had gold earrings in her ears and her makeup was light. She seemed to want to say something.

"What's your name?" I asked.

"Stephanie Reynolds." Her breath made a cloud in the cold air.

"Nice to meet you, Stephanie." I waited.

"Look, I don't want to get into any trouble here," she said at last.

"Do you have something you want to tell me?"

"The police have been hanging around PEDH. Asking questions. About Maureen."

"Yes."

"Well, I don't go to PEDH, see? I go to school in Belleville. So no one's asked me about her."

"That doesn't matter. If you know something, you need to speak to a detective."

"You'll do. You're with the police, right?"

"Yes, but I'm not a detective."

"Doesn't matter. Look, if my parents find out, they'll freak, okay? Promise you won't tell my parents?"

"Stephanie, I can't promise you anything without knowing what you have to tell me. Do you know something about Maureen's death?"

Two boys climbed the steps.

"Hi, Steph," one said.

 Stephanie edged away from the entrance. I followed. The boys opened the door and went inside.

She dropped her voice to a whisper. "I don't know anything about how she died. It's just that...well, I've heard that the cops know she left home. They're trying to find out where she's been staying, right?"

"Do you know?"

"Yeah. I do. She ran away from her house three weeks ago. Her dad was drinking, and her parents started fighting.

Normal stuff at that house, but Maureen figured she'd had enough, you know?"

I could understand that.

"She said she didn't want her baby being exposed to all the bad stuff that went down at her house." Stephanie looked at me, waiting for a reaction.

"We know she was pregnant," I said.

Stephanie nodded. "She was staying at my place."

I'd guessed that.

"My parents have gone to Florida for a month. They go every winter. This is the first year that my aunt Susan hasn't come to stay with me. I'm in grade eleven, so Mom and Dad figured I'm old enough to look after the house. They told me I could have a friend or two sleep over on the weekends. But no one could stay more than one night at a time. No boys and no parties."

She dug into her Roots bag and pulled out a pack of cigarettes. Stephanie dressed as if she had money. If her parents could spend a month in Florida in the winter, they probably did. Seemed a strange friend for the down-and-out Maureen.

"You must have been good friends," I said. "Even though you didn't go to the same school."

She lit her cigarette. She took a deep drag. "Couple of months ago we were having trouble with the computer at home. My dad thought he could fix it. It kept getting worse. I had a really important project due, so I came here to use the computers. Maureen helped me. I liked her. She was tough, but smart." Stephanie took a tissue out of her coat pocket. She blew her nose. "She was nice. We weren't friends, really. But we hung out sometimes. When she left her house that night, she phoned me. Said she needed a place to stay."

I pulled out my cell phone. "Stephanie, you have to tell the detectives about this.

It could be important. I'm going to call someone right now, okay?"

She grimaced. "My parents'll freak."

"I'm sure they'll understand."

I phoned the office and told them I had information for Sergeant Malan. They said they'd let him know.

I should have left it at that. But I had questions too.

"Do you know who got her pregnant?" I asked.

Stephanie wiped her eyes. "No. She said they weren't ready to tell yet. But soon everyone would know. She was happy about it. Excited. About a week before she died, she came home wearing a pretty new ring. He'd given it to her. Something until he could buy a real engagement ring."

"It was blue," I said. "A big blue stone."

"That's right. I was going to be a bridesmaid. I bought her a whole stack of magazines, and we had fun picking out wedding dresses and cakes and stuff."

"Did anyone come around when she was staying with you? Her boyfriend, I mean?"

"No. She went out to meet him."

Didn't sound like much of a boyfriend to me. A cheap blue ring and a bunch of promises. Poor Maureen. Alone and pregnant.

"The night she died?" I asked. "Did she go out with this boyfriend?"

Stephanie threw her unfinished cigarette into the snowbank. "I don't know. I wasn't home. I play hockey, and we had a team party after practice that night. I got home around eleven and Maureen wasn't there." She sobbed. "I heard the news the next morning." Fat tears ran down her face. She didn't lift a hand to wipe them away.

My phone rang. Sergeant Malan, asking where I was.

CHAPTER SIX

The next day I went to Prince Edward District High as school was getting out. I'd gone to this school. I'd graduated only seven years ago. I opened the big doors and walked through the halls, feeling as if I had never been away. I knew my way around without asking directions.

It was snowing heavily. The school floors were dirty with melting snow. I went to the grade-eleven hallway. Groups of girls and boys were standing around the lockers. Talking and flirting. One locker stood out from the rest. It had bunches of plastic flowers stuck to it. Three teddy bears with bright red bows tied around their necks sat on the floor. Cards and messages were taped to the front or stuck into the cracks. Maureen might not have been well liked when she was alive, but sudden death makes anyone popular.

I walked up to a group of girls. "Hi," I said, "I'm Nicole Patterson. I'm with the OPP." That was true. I didn't mention I wasn't part of the investigation team. The girls looked at me. They did not smile. I might have gone to this school a few years ago, but I wasn't one of them any longer. I was an adult. I was a cop.

An outsider.

Someone not to be trusted.

"Did you know Maureen Grey?" I asked.

They nodded. One of the girls lifted a tissue to her eyes. "Hi. I'm Jenny." She was small and plump. Her hair was died jet black.

Sniffled -

Her nail polish was black and she wore too much makeup. "Maureen was so great. Everyone absolutely loved her." She sniffled and blew her nose.

Her friends muttered their agreement. I saw a teacher heading toward us. Mr. MacDonald. He'd been my math teacher in grades eleven and twelve. He was very fat and told bad jokes. None of us had liked him. He opened his mouth to ask who I was. Then he recognized me. "Nancy," he said. "How nice to see you."

"Nicole."

"Right. Nicole." He gave an embarrassed laugh. "How are you? Back for a visit?"

"Yes."

"That's nice," he said. He walked away. I turned back to the kids with a shrug. *(Shoulder)* "Had him for math. Hard marker."

They laughed.

41

"Tell me about Maureen," I said. I didn't know what to ask. None of these kids was going to confess to killing her.

"She was nice," Jenny repeated. "Everyone liked her. I can't believe she's gone."

"Popular, eh?"

"Oh yeah," one of the others girls said, "with the boys."

"What does that mean?"

"Everyone's crying and saying how sad they are. Come on, Jenny, get real. You couldn't stand the bitch," one girl said.

Jenny looked shocked. "That's not true, Cheryl."

"White trash, I think you called her."

"I did not. Well, maybe that once. When she went after Keith even though she knew I liked him."

"It was nothing personal," Cheryl said. She was blond and thin and pretty, with a mouth outlined in deep-red lipstick.

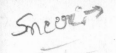

The sneer on her face made her look mean. "Maureen went after anything with a cock."

A boy wandered over to join us. He was big and unattractive and walked with a swagger. His long hair was badly cut and needed a wash. His ears stuck out to the side and pimples dotted his chin. "You talking about Maureen? Cheap slut. Lousy screw."

Jenny gasped. The other girls gave embarrassed laughs. I turned to face him. "Did you sleep with Maureen?"

His eyes narrowed. "Didn't everyone?"

I guessed he was lying. But what do I know? I'm just a probationary constable.

"Come on, Matt. Maureen's dead. Murdered. Be nice," Jenny said.

"Yeah, okay. She was a good screw. I'll be late for practice." He walked away.

The girls watched him go.

"Can you think of any reason," I said, "why anyone would kill Maureen?"

They shook their heads. They were beginning to edge away from me. Bored with my questions.

"We spoke to that sergeant guy already," Cheryl said. "Everyone in class was interviewed. Can't you read his notes or something?"

"Sometimes," I said, "it helps to have a fresh view."

"Whatever. Well, okay. Maureen was a cheap slut. Came to school one day in a new sweater. Only it wasn't new, was it? My older sister, who goes to Loyalist College, had given it to the Second Time Around Shop." The girls all broke into laughter. Even Jenny couldn't disguise a grin.

(Hide)

No doubt Cheryl had been quick to tell everyone where Maureen had bought her new sweater.

"How about the time she had her hair cut?" Jenny said, forgetting she was

44

supposed to be sad. "Looked like her mom had done it and the scissors slipped."

"I didn't say anything to that sergeant," Cheryl said. "But you're a girl, so you'll get it. Maureen's father's a drunk, and her mother got fired from that restaurant by the harbor because they said she was stealing from the till. They were on welfare, and Maureen got her clothes from the secondhand shop."

"Did she have a job?"

"Nah. There's work in summer when the tourists are here. Not much for any of us the rest of the year."

"Her parents told the police she wasn't living at home. Do you know where she was staying?" I knew, of course, from Stephanie. I just wondered if this bunch knew.

"The other cop asked us that. If I cared what miserable Maureen was up to, I might have known. But I didn't." Cheryl looked at the other girls. "We didn't. Did we?"

No, they agreed. Clearly Cheryl was the boss here.

"Thanks for your help," I said.

"Sure." They shifted their backpacks and purses and began to edge away.

"Are you going to give us your card? Like if we remember something?" Cheryl asked.

"Speak to Sergeant Malan," I said. Up until now I was just asking some questions. Like anyone might do. If I started handing out my business card, I could get in real trouble for interfering where I wasn't supposed to.

The girls swung their hips and tossed their hair as they walked away.

Poor Maureen, I thought. High School. Toughest place on earth, sometimes.

I followed the girls around the corner, thinking I'd go out the back way to my car. I couldn't find the door. They'd built an extension onto the school since my time here. I had to circle around.

There was only one person in the grade-eleven corridor when I got back. A boy stood in front of the flower- and teddy-bear-decorated locker. His head was down, and he held his right palm pressed up against the metal door. He was dressed in jeans and a short-sleeved blue shirt. He was about six feet tall and well built, with heavy shoulders and muscular arms. His black hair was cut very short.

I started to say something. To ask him why he was here and what he knew about Maureen.

But before I got close, a boy approached him. He was dressed in gym clothes. His running shoes were the size of boats. He carried a bulging sports bag. "The fuck you doin', Jason?" he said. "Mr. Bowen won't be happy if you're late."

I slipped back so I was standing out of sight against the wall.

"Go without me, Mark."

"No. You've been off your game all week. Bowen's scheduled a special weight session and he won't be pleased if you miss it."

"Fuck Bowen."

Mark put his hand on Jason's back. Jason shrugged it off with a warning growl. They paid no attention to me standing in the shadows.

"Come on, man. The girl's dead. But you're not. Get over it."

Jason's body tensed. Then his shoulders relaxed, and he said, "Yeah, okay. Go ahead. I'll get my stuff and be there in a minute. Tell Mr. Bowen I had to stay behind in English class for a few minutes."

Mark gave him a hearty slap on the back. "Great. And stop moping about. Bowen'll call you a wimp if he sees that look on your face."

Jason walked away. Mark watched him go, a smile turning up the edges of his mouth.

CHAPTER SEVEN

I saw the same bunch of kids a couple of days later at Maureen's funeral.

My mom wanted to pay her respects, so I went with her. Sergeant Malan and Detective Roberts were there. They stood to one side, watching everyone.

The funeral was well attended. That's normal for a young person and a sudden, dramatic death. The girls in her class might not have liked Maureen, but they wouldn't pass up the chance to look sad. Or to get an afternoon off class. I recognized most of the group I'd spoken to the other day at the school.

Mr. and Mrs. Grey were there, of course. She cried throughout the brief service. He sat beside her, scowling at everyone. He wore a white shirt and thin black tie. She wore a black skirt with a gray blouse. The blouse had a coffee stain on the front. Mrs. Grey had a large purple-and-black bruise on the side of her face. As Paul Malan had said, we all knew the Greys. There's nothing much we can do if she won't tell anyone her husband knocked her around.

There wouldn't be a public graveside service. Instead we went downstairs to the basement of the funeral home. Coffee and tea, sandwiches and cookies had been laid out. Mr. Grey had disappeared. Mrs. Grey stood alone in a dark corner. Her eyes were very red, and her nose was swollen.

bruise :—

She clutched a clump of damp and torn tissues in her hand.

Mom and I went over to her. Mom told her that Maureen had been a whiz on the computer. She often helped the other kids if they were having trouble.

"Thank you," Mrs. Grey said. "She was a good girl. She wanted to be a computer programmer when she finished school."

Mom went to talk to some of her friends from the youth center. I saw Sergeant Malan standing by himself, drinking a cup of tea. "Where's Mr. Grey?" I asked.

"In a bar most likely. Roberts is keeping an eye on him."

"You think he did it?"

"We don't think anything," Malan said. "We're keeping an eye on him, that's all. What are you doing here? You're not involved in the case."

"I came with my mom."

He finished his tea and walked away.

Jason, the boy I'd seen at Maureen's locker, was standing alone. He was very good-looking. He wore a gray suit, a tie with thin blue stripes, and a white shirt. He had a glass of orange juice in one hand and a Nanaimo bar in the other. His eyes and nose were red.

Some of the kids had their parents with them. During the service I'd noticed a man in a very good suit sitting beside Jason. The man was now on the other side of the room. He was talking to one of the mothers.

I went up to the boy. "Hi, I'm Nicole Patterson."

"Jason Fitzpatrick. Are you a grief counselor?"

"No. I'm with the OPP."

"You're young to be a detective."

I didn't correct him. "Were you friends with Maureen?"

He looked around. His father was still talking to the woman. "I knew her from school."

"Jason, how are you?"

"I'm okay, Mrs. Patterson."

My mom had joined us.

"I don't see you at the center much these days."

He shrugged. "Just busy." He had big shoulders and large hands.

"Have you decided yet where you're going to go next year? It must be so exciting for you."

"Yeah. I guess. No, I haven't decided. Dad has some ideas."

"I sure do." Mr. Fitzpatrick slapped his son on the back. Jason scowled. "But it isn't up to me, is it? My boy'll make the right choice."

I had no idea what they were talking about.

"If you'll excuse me, I want to extend my condolences to Mrs. Grey." Jason left us. His head was down.

Mr. Fitzpatrick watched him go. "Tragic business," he said. "But I can't say I'm surprised."

"Surprised at what?" Mom asked.

"Maureen. Getting herself killed." He lowered his voice. "Girl like that. Family like that. Look at her mother. Couldn't be bothered to wear a clean blouse to her daughter's funeral. And her face. Guess she walked into a door, eh?" He laughed. It was a very ugly laugh.

My mom looked angry. "We don't choose our parents, Brian. Maureen was a nice girl who'd been given a bad lot in life."

"I'm sure you think so." He smiled at her.

"I do. Now, when will Jason be back at the center? He was going to help me with our grant application."

"I don't think he'll be coming back. He's done his required volunteer service. For the next couple of months he has to concentrate on his schoolwork and staying in shape. I think we've been polite enough for one day. Time to go."

Mom and I watched him walk over to where his son stood with Mrs. Grey. He took Jason by the arm and said something. Then they left the room. Jason didn't say goodbye to any of the other young people. His father didn't speak to Mrs. Grey.

"When I said we can't choose our parents," Mom said, "I wasn't only talking about Maureen. Jason's helped us a lot at the center. His father only cares about what people can do for him."

"Was Jason close friends with Maureen? Like a boyfriend, I mean?"

"I never saw them together, but I don't think so. I doubt his father would have allowed it. He only let Jason come to the center because the boy needs the volunteer hours to graduate."

"Hi, Mrs. Patterson." It was Stephanie. She looked nice in a black suit and white blouse. Her eye makeup was smudged. She twisted a damp tissue in her fingers. Mom and Stephanie chatted for a few minutes. Stephanie had been interviewed by Sergeant Malan after I phoned him and told him where Maureen had been staying. She hadn't been able to tell him anything more than she had told me. Malan had told her to talk to her parents, and they were on their way home from Florida.

Stephanie said goodbye and left. Mom went off to chat with one of her friends. I saw Sergeant Malan answer his cell phone. He didn't look happy.

"Problem?" I said when he'd hung up.

"Lab report on Maureen's scarf. The only skin samples were from her."

"Her attacker would probably have been wearing gloves."

"Yes. It wouldn't have looked strange. Anyone would have had gloves on a cold night like that one."

"Maureen didn't."

"I noticed that."

Malan glanced at the clock on the wall. "Roberts called to tell me that Grey's sitting on a stool in a bar. Two o'clock in the afternoon. The day of his daughter's funeral. You asked me earlier if I thought he'd done it. Yes, I do. I'm convinced Pete Grey murdered his daughter. I just can't prove it. Not yet. But I will." He put his cell phone away and left the room. He looked very angry.

I found my mom and said it was time to leave.

CHAPTER EIGHT

I'd been given time off work to take Mom to Maureen's funeral. I drove her back to the youth center where she'd left her car. Then I went to the station. I put my uniform on and headed out onto the road. It was snowing lightly. Big fat flakes. The radio said there'd be a storm tonight. We'd be busy then. We always were when it snowed.

We patrol the cemeteries a lot. At night when the drunks are out and looking to make trouble. Even in the daytime. Cemeteries are good places for kids to go drinking and for drug deals to go down.

Glenwood Cemetery's located very close to town. It's a beautiful place with big trees and lots of history. I drove down the steep hill and through the grounds slowly. Just looking around. The trees were covered in new snow. Everything was pure and white and very pretty. There was no wind.

On a hill in the distance, I could see a mound of earth. I drove over to have a look. A new grave. No headstone yet and the flowers piled on the ground were still fresh. The snow was marked by tire tracks and footprints.

They'd buried Maureen here. Everyone had left, and it was still and quiet.

Everyone, except for Jason Fitzpatrick. He was wrapped in a good winter coat. A wool scarf was around his neck and leather gloves were on his hands.

He didn't look up as the black-and-white OPP patrol car came to a stop. I got out and put on my hat and my own gloves. I walked over to him.

"Everything okay?" I asked.

He jumped in surprise.

"Sorry," he said. "I didn't hear you, Officer. What'd you say?"

"I asked if everything's all right here."

He looked at me closely. I look so different when I'm in uniform that most people don't recognize me. "Didn't I see you earlier, at the funeral home?"

"I was there. My mom's Mrs. Patterson from the youth center. I'm Constable Patterson."

"Hi."

"Jason," I said. "Were you and Maureen close?"

His eyes were wet. I thought he'd been crying.

"No," he said. He pulled a crumpled tissue out of his pocket and blew his nose. "I hardly knew her. She was just a girl from school and the youth center. She was good with computers. Helped me out once when my laptop crashed. I'm sorry she died. That's all. They say her father killed her."

"Do you know anything about that?"

"Nah. Just what people are saying."

He turned to leave. A shiny red Toyota Echo was parked on the path.

As I've said, I'm not a detective. I'm just a probationary constable. I could get in trouble for interfering with the investigation.

But I had a thought, and I couldn't let it go.

"I was the one who found her, you know," I said. He kept walking. His head was down against the wind. "I found a ring. A pretty ring, with a big blue stone. It was lying on the ground beside her. It might have fallen off as she struggled." He stopped. Snow fell on his shoulders.

"Do you know anything about that ring, Jason?"

He turned and looked at me. "I've seen it. She wore it to school. She thought it was pretty. Girls like that sort of thing."

"It was pretty."

"What happened to it?"

"They gave it to her mom," I said. I glanced at the freshly turned soil. Had Maureen worn it to her grave?

His face twisted in pain. He let out a small sob. He wiped his glove across his eyes. When he looked at me again his eyes were dry.

"That's good," he said.

"She didn't seem to have many friends. I'm glad you were her friend. My mom says Maureen got a rotten deal out of life."

"Life's tough sometimes." The snow was falling faster now. The air smelled of newly dug earth. "Be seeing you around, Constable."

He wiped flakes of snow off the window of the red Echo with his hand. He got into the car and drove away.

I stood by Maureen Grey's grave for a long time. Snow fell around me. My radio called me to Main Street. A woman had slipped on the ice in front of the library and couldn't get up.

CHAPTER NINE

I got to the library at the same time as the ambulance. The lady was eighty years old and had broken her left arm. I could see pain in the lines in her face, but she tried to be cheerful. She thanked the paramedics and me for our trouble.

I didn't wait until my shift was over before going to my parents' house. It was almost dark when I got to the farm. The sun had gone down, and in the west the sky was streaked with color. The snow on the fields glowed pink. Trixie, Mom's big shaggy golden retriever, was very excited to see me.

"This is a surprise," Mom said. She looked past me to the cruiser. Dad had finished plowing the driveway. He'd have to do it again soon.

"I need to talk to you about Jason Fitzpatrick and Maureen Grey, Mom. Can I come in?"

"Of course you can come in."

We went into the kitchen. A big pot of soup was on the stove and bread was in the oven. The house smelled wonderful. Just like it had when I was growing up here. Now that I'm living on my own, I try to cook sometimes. But it's too easy to stop at McDonalds or a pizza place and grab something. I sat down at the big wooden table, and Mom put the kettle on. I glanced outside. The deck lights shone on outdoor furniture, piled high with snow.

"What about Jason and Maureen?" Mom asked. She put teacups, milk and sugar on the table.

"I'm pretty sure they were together. I bet he got her pregnant."

Mom sat down without making the tea. "I try not to listen to gossip, but girls whispered stories about Maureen. They said she slept with just about any boy who asked."

"Teenage girls can be mean," I said.

"They had to have had a grain of truth to work with."

"Not really. They can smell weakness like a shark smells blood. Maureen was poor and from a family that's the talk of the town. An easy target. Do you know she slept around? Or is that just what you heard?"

Mom sat silently, looking out at the snow. "You're right, dear. Sometimes I take things too much at face value. Last year a boy touched her breast when she was showing him to the computers. She told him off and wasn't shy about it."

"You see."

"But the fact is she was pregnant. She was sleeping with someone. Once at least. No one has come forward to say he was her boyfriend. So maybe her reputation was true, Nicole. Sad as that is. Why do you think it might be Jason?"

"I saw him at her locker. Then at the funeral home and later at the cemetery. He's really sad."

Mom sighed. "Jason's a rich, spoiled boy."

"What does that have to do with anything?"

"These boys," Mom said, shaking her head. "Jason has his own car. It was a birthday present from his parents. They're not from around here. The family moved to the County a year ago. His father owns the company that's building those new houses outside of town. Lots of people are not happy at them digging up all that lakefront for their big fancy houses. Cutting down lovely old trees."

"So?"

Mom shook her head. "Doesn't matter. Jason could be nice, I'll say that. Very charming. But he's an outsider and not many people in the County have the sort of money his family does. He's good-looking and the star of the football team. I've heard that he's been offered scholarships from some American universities."

"Really?"

"He's in the papers all the time. Jason's a very big fish in the small pond that's Prince Edward District High."

The radio at my shoulder crackled. I held my hand up for Mom to be quiet. But the call wasn't for me.

"Boys like Jason," Mom continued, "with everything—fame, money, ambition. Handsome football stars. They don't fall in love with girls like Maureen. You should know that, Nicole. Sex, maybe. But not love." Mom shook her head sadly.

Trixie nuzzled at her hand. Mom scratched behind the dog's floppy ears.

"I think you're wrong, Mom. I think Jason really cared about her. I saw his face at the cemetery. He was crying."

"Sure, he's sad now. She's dead. Didn't mean he wouldn't have dumped her and then laughed at her after."

Trixie whined.

"Perhaps he's more than sad," Mom said, slowly as if she was letting a thought out before it was finished. "Maybe he's sorry. Feeling guilty? Have you thought about that, Nicole? Maybe she was demanding money. Maybe he killed her because she was going to ruin his ambitions."

I thought about Jason. Standing at Maureen's locker. The funeral. Later at the cemetery, alone in the snow. "I don't see it, Mom. How could she ruin his ambitions? In this day and age, no one's going to care that he got a girl pregnant. If he did. Just the opposite. His pals'd think he's a real man. It's not as if there has to be a shotgun wedding or anything. Okay, Maureen's life might fall off the rails if she decides to continue with the pregnancy and keep the baby. But Jason? Even if she wanted money for support, you said his family can afford it. More likely he'd just go away to school in the States and forget all about her and her baby."

"Maureen's father?" Mom said. "Everyone in town knows what he's like. A drunk layabout, abusive. Maybe he saw a chance to get some money out of the Fitzpatrick family and argued with Jason?"

"Why would Jason kill Maureen, then? That makes no sense. More likely he'd go after Pete Grey. It wouldn't be too hard to murder him. Provoke him into taking a swing and claim self-defense."

"Have you considered that Pete might have killed Maureen?"

"Yeah. That's what Sergeant Malan thinks. He's watching Pete, but he can't find any evidence. Don't tell anyone I told you that. It's confidential."

Mom laughed. "Everyone in the County knows, dear."

"I can't see a reason for Pete to kill his daughter. Maybe in a drunken fight. But she wasn't beaten up or anything. She was taken by surprise and strangled."

"Could he have been angry at her for getting pregnant, perhaps?"

"Gee, Mom. This is the twenty-first century. No one cares about a girl's reputation. The Greys don't have a reputation worth protecting anyway."

A gust of wind rattled the glass doors to the deck. I looked outside. Snow was blowing across the fields.

"Kettle's gone cold," Mom said. "Shall I turn it back on, dear?"

"No, thanks, Mom. It looks like that storm's moving in. Better get back on the road."

We stood up. I put my hat on my head. "Bye, Trixie," I said.

Mom walked with me to the door. "Poor Maureen," she said. "She was smarter and kinder than anyone let her be. It makes me so mad sometimes. The way the other girls laughed at her. The way the boys made her the butt of their jokes. Boys like Jason Fitzpatrick."

"Night, Mom," I said. I went back to my car and headed toward town. Before long, the radio called. Car accident on County Road 10. Injuries. I switched on lights and sirens and sped up. I drove through Cherry Valley. Flashing blue and red lights reflected off falling snow.

Mom was wrong.

I'd seen Jason's face at the cemetery.

He hadn't killed her.

CHAPTER TEN

It had been a very bad accident. Two men in one car were seriously injured. One was trapped and screaming in fear and pain. Firefighters had to cut the side of the car away to get him out. A man and woman in the other vehicle were bruised and shook-up. Someone had been driving too fast. Icy roads, strong winds, blowing snow.

Happens all the time.

Larry Johnstone and I went to the Bean Counter on Main Street for a quick coffee after the scene was cleared. I wondered, sometimes, if he liked me. But I wasn't looking for a relationship right now. I had my career to think about.

We got our coffees and settled at a vacant table. The place was largely empty so we could talk quietly.

"You've been helping the detectives with that murder on Kingsley Road," Larry said. He took a big bite out of his cookie.

"I wish," I said. "No, I haven't been helping. Just asking a few questions of people I know."

"Sounds like helping to me."

I shrugged. "The sergeant's from the city. He doesn't have local contacts. I've lived here all my life. I know a lot of people. My mom knows almost everyone."

"Why do you care?" He popped the last piece of the cookie into his mouth.

I sipped my coffee. His eyes were fixed on my face, his expression serious.

"Because I'm a police officer and someone's been murdered. It's my job to care.
Don't you, Larry?"

He licked crumbs off his fingers.
"Yeah, I want to catch the bastard who did
that to her. But you...I think there's something deeper. I think there's something
almost personal."

"Well there isn't," I snapped. "I didn't
know the girl. Never met her. Never talked
to her."

"If you say so."

Clearly Larry didn't believe me. I wasn't
sure if I believed myself.

I'd known a girl like Maureen when I
was in high school. Her name was Alison
Savage. She also came from a family down
on their luck. Alison's family problems
were not booze and violence. Her father
was disabled and her mother was mentally
ill. The family lived in social housing.

They didn't have much money to spend on clothes and things for their three kids. Alison was not pretty. She had a large nose and bad skin and was overweight. Of course, the kids called her "The Savage." We made what we thought were jungle noises around her.

In grade ten Alison and I were teamed for a science project. She was smart and eager to do well. She did almost all the work on our project. We got an A-plus and an award at the science fair. And I found that I liked her. We became friends.

I've always been good at sports, and I was popular in high school. I hung around with the pretty girls, the rich girls, the in girls. When I made friends with Alison, my crowd were amused at first and then shocked.

They told me I had to decide between them or her.

And so I dumped her.

I won't forget the look on her face when she came into the library and sat beside me.

She gave me a big smile and said, "Hi." I didn't say anything. I gathered my books, stood up and went to another table.

Where the girls whose approval I needed and I put our heads together and giggled.

Alison bent her head over her books. She tried hard not to cry.

Not long after that, Alison went to a party with one of the grade-twelve boys.

On Monday, word spread through the school like wildfire that a group of boys—and some grown men—had raped her. She missed some school. When she came back she had fading bruises and cuts on her face and hands. The girls, including me, said she'd been asking for it.

We walked into English class to see that someone had written on the board, *Alison has a savage pussy.*

The teacher was furious, but we all read it before she erased the words.

That night Alison killed herself. She took an overdose of her father's pain medication.

Maybe now I was trying to make up for the harm I'd done Alison by seeking justice for Maureen.

"If you're finished," I said to Larry, "let's go."

Larry headed back to the station to do some paperwork. I drove through town and was passing the harbor when I got another call.

"Three-oh. One-oh-two?" That was me.

"Go ahead."

Dispatch sent me to a fight that had broken out in a bar in town. I took off toward the scene, under full lights and sirens.

I parked half on the sidewalk and pushed my way through the crowd gathered outside. Bernie's was a cheap, run-down bar. The lighting was bad, and the furniture worn and scratched. It smelled of spilled liquor, stale cooking grease and anger.

Country music, played too loud, came from speakers mounted on the walls. A couple of chairs were overturned. Broken glass sparkled on the floor.

Most fist fights don't last long. Not when it's a couple of middle-aged men. Overweight and out of shape. They take one or two swings at each other and they're too tired to do anything more. By the time I arrived it was mostly over.

The bartender was holding a base-ball bat in one hand and a phone in the other. A woman stood against the wall, screaming. Whether in support or in fear I couldn't tell. Probably both. A man stood in the center of the room. He gripped a beer bottle with the neck broken off. He waved it in front of him, yelling and swearing a blue streak. Another man had blood streaming down his face from a cut above his eye. His dirty white sweatshirt was covered in blood.

I took one look at the broken bottle and called for backup. "Why don't you put that down," I said from the doorway.

The man turned his head slowly and looked at me. "Why?"

It was Pete Grey. He was still dressed in the suit he'd worn to his daughter's funeral. His words were slurred and he swayed on his feet.

"Because I'm telling you to," I said. I took a step forward. I was careful to stay out of his reach. I felt for the pepper spray on my belt.

The woman stopped screaming. She watched us with wide eyes. My radio told me backup was on its way.

The bartender said, "Do what the lady says, Pete, and I'll forget about it. No problem. Ed here was way outta line. Weren't ya, Ed?"

Ed mumbled something. The woman nodded.

"You've just come from your daughter's funeral, Mr. Grey," I said. "Do you want to spend the night in jail? You should be at home with your wife."

He lowered the bottle. But he didn't put it down. "Maureen was my girl. She was a good girl."

"My mother knew her," I said. "Mom says Maureen was smart and nice. Mom liked her a lot."

"I taught her to ride a bike when she was little," Grey said. "I ran along behind her holding on to the seat. Didn't go more than a few yards before she had the hang of it and didn't need my help. She got good marks in school too."

"Put the bottle down, Mr. Grey, and tell me about Maureen. She was pretty, wasn't she?" I heard sirens. Blue and red light washed the dingy bar. The door opened with a blast of cold air. I felt an officer standing behind me.

Pete Grey looked at me. His eyes were full of pain. "Real pretty. Maureen was a good girl," he said again.

"Yes, sir."

"He…" The bottle swung toward Ed again. "Had no account to say bad things about her."

I didn't like the look in Ed's eyes. I knew him also. Another drunken lowlife. He gave a mean grin. Now that the police were here to take any blow aimed at him, he was full of talk.

"I didn't say nothin' but the truth." Ed glanced at the woman, hoping for a laugh. "I heard she was pregnant. Shouldn't bother you none, Pete. Not as if she was your daughter anyway. Like mother, like daughter, I guess." He wiped a drop of blood away with the back of his hand.

Pete lifted the bottle. "You pack of shit."

"Shut the hell up," I yelled at Ed. "Or I'll arrest you for inciting violence."

Ed lifted his hands and backed away. "Hey, just tellin' the truth here. No hard feelings."

"Get out," I said. "Now."

"Sure, sure." He stayed against the walls and edged around me out the door.

The woman followed Ed. Pete Grey watched them go.

He put the broken bottle onto the counter. I let out a long breath I hadn't noticed I was holding.

"She was my girl," he said. "Maybe I wasn't much of a father to her, but I loved her. She knew I loved her. She was going to have a baby. A beautiful little girl just like my Maureen. I would have taken care of them. I would have made a good grandpa."

"I'm sure you would," I said.

"Some bastard killed her." Grey started to sob. His whole body shook. He leaned against the bar, crying for what he had lost.

"Come on," I said. "I'll take you home."

CHAPTER ELEVEN

I drove Pete Grey home. He cried the whole way. I could see his wife standing at the front window as I helped him out of the car. She opened the door and took him into her arms. I stood in the snow, feeling awful.

The light was on in the detectives' office when I got back to the station. I shook snow off my hat and jacket. Stomped more snow off my boots. I popped coins into the pop machine. A can of Coke fell out. I pulled the tab and took a long drink.

Sergeant Malan sat at his desk, typing on the computer. I knocked on the open door. He looked up. He had dark circles under his eyes. "Yes?" he said.

I told him about the incident with Pete Grey. He took off his glasses and rubbed his eyes.

"I believe him, sir," I said. It wasn't my place to tell a detective what I thought. But I knew I had to say something. "I don't think Pete killed his Maureen."

"Probably not," Malan agreed. "Right now I don't have much in the way of suspects."

I swallowed. "Well...uh...I've been thinking."

He pushed back his chair. "Not your job to think, Constable. After ten years on the job, you're allowed to think."

"Oh," I said. "Sorry."

He laughed. "Get me one of those." He pointed to the can of Coke in my hand. "And then you can tell me what's up."

I got his drink and hurried back. I hoped I wouldn't be called out by dispatch again. Not before I could say what I wanted to say.

"I know it's not really my job, Sergeant," I began.

"But?" he said.

"How did you know I'm going to say but?"

"Eager young officers always have ideas. Go ahead."

"Maureen Grey."

"What about her?"

"I'm local, right? I've lived in the County all my life. My mom's heavily involved in the community. She volunteers at the youth center. She knew Maureen."

The sergeant hadn't offered me a chair. I shifted from one foot to the other. My boots dripped melting snow onto the carpet.

"I think a boy named Jason Fitzpatrick knows something about her death."

Malan linked his fingers together. "Fitzpatrick. I remember him. We interviewed the kids at her school. He said they weren't friends."

"That's not true. They dated."

"Who told you this?"

I felt my cheeks turn red. "Actually, no one told me. I guessed."

"You guessed?"

"You saw him at her funeral. The big good-looking boy in the nice suit. Remember how sad he was?"

"Everyone was sad, Constable. It was a funeral." The sergeant began to turn back to his computer.

"They were pretending to be sad. The kids, I mean. They didn't like her while she was alive. They laughed at her because the family's on welfare and her father's a drunk. They only care about her death so they can be part of the drama. But Jason really was sad. I saw him later, at the cemetery.

When everyone else had left. He was the only one who stayed. He shouldn't have been there anyway. The burial was private."

"Thank you, Constable. If I think of anything more, I'll ask you."

"You don't have a suspect, do you?" I blurted out, "It wasn't Mr. Grey. If he'd killed her, it wouldn't be any mystery. He would have got mad and bashed her brains in."

He swung his chair back around to face me. "That's true, Nicole. You think this boy Jason killed her. Why?"

"She was pregnant. He got her pregnant."

"Happens all the time. No reason to kill her."

"I know that. See, sir, I don't think Jason killed her. I think he was in love with her. I saw his face at the cemetery. He gave her that ring, the one with the blue stone. Sure, it was just a cheap thing, but it meant something to both of them. Someone else killed her. Because Jason was in love with her."

"Who?"

"I don't know. I thought I'd mention it, that's all."

He gave me a tight smile. "Thank you, Nicole. You've given me something to think about." He looked at his watch. "It's not too late to make a call." He got to his feet. "You can drive me."

"Where?"

"I want to talk to Jason Fitzpatrick again. Sounds like he lied when he said he hardly knew Maureen. I wonder what else he might have lied about."

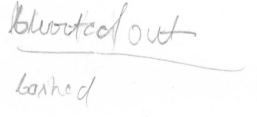

blurted out

barked

CHAPTER TWELVE

The Fitzpatricks lived on Highway 33, heading east toward the Glenora Ferry. The long winding driveway passed big oak trees. The lawn was a wide expanse of untouched snow running down to the lake. The small harbor was dark, but lights twinkled from houses on the opposite shore. It was still snowing as I pulled up in front of a large modern house. All wood and glass.

Plenty of money.

I rang the doorbell. It was opened by an attractive woman in her forties. It was after nine o'clock, but she was dressed in a tailored suit, stockings and pumps, and nice jewelry. Her makeup was perfect. Her blond hair was expensively cut and colored.

"May I help you?" she asked. Her words were slightly slurred. I suspected she'd been drinking.

Sergeant Malan introduced us and showed his ID. He said he wanted to speak to her son, Jason.

She blinked in confusion but opened the door. The house smelled of furniture polish and the woman's expensive perfume. A man came out of a side door. He carried a crystal glass half full of a smoky brown liquid and cubes of fresh ice.

"What's this about?" Brian Fitzpatrick asked.

"I'm Sergeant Paul Malan. I'm investigating the death of Maureen Grey and would like to speak to your son, Jason. I believe Jason knew the dead girl."

Fitzpatrick's eyes flicked across my face. He didn't recognize me from the funeral this afternoon. "Jason went to the same school as Maureen. So did a lot of kids. Are you planning on paying a nighttime visit to them all?"

"Is Jason at home?" Malan asked.

"Yes, I'm here." The boy stood at the top of the basement stairs. He was dressed in a pair of sweat pants and a PEDH T-shirt. A towel was tossed over his broad shoulders. His hair was wet and his shirt was damp. He was breathing heavily. He'd been working out.

His eyes widened when he saw me, but he said nothing.

"I want to talk to you about Maureen Grey," Malan asked. "May we have a seat?"

"Come in, please," Mrs. Fitzpatrick said.

"No," Mr. Fitzpatrick said at the same time. "Go back to your program, Leslie," he told his wife. "I'll handle this."

The woman nodded and slipped down the hall. A door opened and I could hear the sound of a TV. Then the door shut and all was quiet.

Malan turned to the boy. "Jason, when I interviewed you at school you said you didn't know Maureen Grey other than as someone you saw around."

"Yeah." The boy glanced at his father out of the corner of his eyes.

"Is that true?" Malan asked.

"If my son said it, then it's true," Fitzpatrick said. "Now, it's getting late and Jason has school tomorrow. He's in grade twelve, and we have hopes of a good scholarship. He has to keep his marks up."

"Football player, are you?" Malan asked.

I shifted the heavy weight of my gun belt. I was very warm in the overheated house in my winter uniform jacket. No one paid any attention to me.

"Yes," Jason answered.

"Pretty good player, I hear."

"That has nothing to do with anything. Good night, Sergeant," Brian Fitzpatrick repeated.

"Pretty good, yeah," Jason said with a touch of pride in his voice.

"What was your relationship with Maureen Grey?"

"They had no relationship," Fitzpatrick said quickly. "They went to the same school. They were not even in the same grade. My son was kind enough to go to the girl's funeral and pay his respects. Why are you making something out of that? You should be arresting the girl's father. She was a cheap slut, and her father's a drunken bully."

"She wasn't a slut," Jason said. His handsome face turned dark with anger.

"What I mean"—Fitzpatrick took a deep drink from his glass—"is that the unfortunate young woman was not friends with my son. You've taken up enough of our time." He moved to open the door.

"Is your father right, Jason?" I said. Malan shot me a look. It wasn't my place to say anything. But I couldn't just turn around and leave.

Jason let out a sob. His voice broke as he said, "No. He's not right. I loved her. I loved Maureen. We were going to be married."

"That's nonsense," his father shouted. "You're seventeen years old. You don't know what the hell you're talking about. Now you." He turned to Malan. "Get out of my house."

"I can leave," the sergeant said. "And take Jason down to the station to finish this conversation. Is that what you want?"

"You gave her the ring," I said. "Didn't you, Jason? The ring with the blue stone."

Jason nodded. Tears ran down his handsome face. "It was just a cheap thing.

Something for her to wear until I could buy a real diamond."

"And where the hell did you think you were going to get the money for a diamond ring?" his father snapped.

Jason ignored him. "I know what they said about her. The kids at school. They were wrong. She was a wonderful person. A beautiful girl. I loved her."

"Did you kill her?" Malan asked, very softly.

Jason shook his head. His father sputtered.

"We planned to be married when I finished university," Jason said. "I'd decided not to go to the States to play football. Even though it was what my dad wanted. I've been accepted at Queens University in Kingston. That way I wouldn't be too far away and could come home and see Maureen on the weekends. She'd graduate next year and get a job. Or something."

"Or something," his father spat. "That's a great plan. Or something. How the hell long do you think it would be before the slut started sleeping around on you? A week, a month? While you worked your ass off to support her and her brat. What about football, eh? A top-ranked college in the States. The NFL. All our dreams and hopes."

"Your dreams, Dad. Your hopes. I like playing football, and I'm good at it. But I plan to go into law. That's what I've always wanted to do."

"She got pregnant," I said. "That changed things didn't it, Jason?"

He nodded. "She was having my baby. Our baby. We talked about abortion or adoption, but neither of us wanted that. We wanted to keep it. *We*. We were going to love it and raise it." He looked at his father. Then he leaned against the wall. His broad chest moved with his sobs. "None of it matters anymore. Maureen's gone. The baby's gone. I'll go to your damned college and play fucking football. You can brag to all your friends what a hotshot your son is."

Brian Fitzpatrick lifted his glass and finished the rest of his drink in one gulp. The edges of his mouth turned up in a sly smile. "Of course you will, son. You've got what you wanted, Sergeant. Now, please leave us alone."

"No," Malan said. "I don't have what I wanted. There's still the question of why Maureen died. Jason, do you know anything else you're not telling us?"

Brian Fitzpatrick threw his glass against the wall. It shattered. "Get the hell out of my house," he roared.

Malan nodded to me. I opened the door. A gust of snow and icy wind blew in. "Very well," Malan said. "But this case is still open. Someone killed that young woman and I intend to find out who it was.

Someone who had dreams and hopes and ambitions. And a pregnant schoolgirl from a poor family was standing in the way."

"I didn't kill her, Sergeant Malan," Jason said. His voice was low and very sad. "I loved her. I wanted to be with her forever."

"I'm not thinking of your dreams," Malan said. "Your dreams included Maureen." He looked directly at Brian Fitzpatrick. "But someone else's didn't."

Jason gasped. All the blood drained from his face.

"Don't be ridiculous," Fitzpatrick said.

"I told you," Jason said. "That night, at dinner. I told you I was accepting the offer from Queens and turning down the American ones. I told you Maureen was having a baby."

Fitzpatrick shrugged. "I knew you'd come to your senses soon enough and see that I'm right." He tried to look unconcerned, but a vein throbbed in his forehead.

It was cold, standing in the open door while the snow blew in. Fitzpatrick was starting to sweat.

"I'd been afraid to tell you," Jason said. "I figured you'd yell and carry on. Threaten to cut me off. I told you Maureen was pregnant and we were going to get married in the summer. Mom cried a little bit. She left the table before we were finished. You just kept on eating. You said I'd change my mind."

"And you would have, soon enough."

"Pregnancies have a way of continuing while people make up their minds," I said. "University scholarships don't. Was there a deadline from the American college, Jason? If you turned them down, they wouldn't make the offer again."

Malan lifted a hand, telling me to be quiet.

Jason looked at his father. "The deadline's this week. Now that Maureen's dead, it didn't seem to matter anymore what I did.

I sent in my acceptance yesterday. Mom took pictures of you posing while I signed the papers." He let out a roar. A cry of pure rage and pain.

He flew across the room.

He punched his father full in the face. Fitzpatrick's nose broke in a spray of blood, and he dropped to the floor. Jason pulled back his foot and aimed a kick at his father's head. Before he could connect, I was on him, pulling him off balance. I slid my leg between his, twisted and brought him crashing down.

I stood over him, expecting him to try to get back to his feet. But he rolled up into a ball and lay there, sobbing.

Malan had Fitzpatrick by the arm. He pulled the man to his feet. Mrs. Fitzpatrick stood in the hallway. Her eyes were wide with shock and her hand was pressed to her mouth.

Brian Fitzpatrick spat out a mouthful of blood. More blood streamed down his face.

"I did it for you," he shouted at his son.
"Don't you understand? You were going to
throw your life away on a no-account slut
and her bastard. The kid probably wasn't
even yours. She probably spread her legs
for every boy in that school. Got herself
knocked up. Figured you'd make a good
meal ticket."

"Brian Fitzpatrick," Sergeant Malan
said, "I am arresting you for the murder of
Maureen Grey. It is my duty to…"

I snapped handcuffs on Fitzpatrick's
wrists. He did not look at his son or his wife.

CHAPTER THIRTEEN

Mrs. Fitzpatrick ran for the phone. I gripped her husband's arm and led him outside. I stuffed him into the back of the cruiser. He didn't say anything. Jason lay on the floor and cried.

When we left the Fitzpatrick home, heavy snow was falling. I could hardly see the road in front of my headlights. As I pulled into the police station, we got a call. Another accident. A bad one. A car had gone off the road in Bloomfield and crashed into a group of people coming out of a restaurant. At least one dead.

Some people just can't drive in the freakin' snow.

Johnstone radioed to say he'd take it, but I knew he'd need backup.

I helped Sergeant Malan get Brian Fitzpatrick into a cell. Then I left. I was sorry to have been called away.

* * *

I was off the next day and slept until noon. I made coffee and a bagel with peanut butter and sat down at my computer. Outside my window a bright sun shone in a blue sky. Fresh snow sparkled like chips of glass. We'd gotten more than a foot in the night, and trees sagged under the weight. I finished my breakfast and was checking the news in *The Globe and Mail* when my cell phone rang.

"Are you up?" Paul Malan asked.

"Yes."

"You deserve to hear the results of our interview with Brian Fitzpatrick. Can I come around?"

"Yes, sir," I said. I rushed to get into the shower and get dressed. I was tying my wet hair back when the door buzzer sounded.

Malan had stopped at Miss Lily's Café. He carried two cups of hot coffee and a bag of fresh pastries.

"What happened?" I asked, before he even sat down at the table in my tiny kitchen.

"You did a good job, Nicole. Your instincts were spot-on."

I blushed with pleasure.

He took the top off his coffee cup. Steam rose. He ripped open the paper bag and took out a couple of Danishes and two muffins. "Fitzpatrick made a full confession. By the time his lawyer arrived, he'd told us the whole story. I guess he thought if he explained it all to me, I'd understand."

I took a bran muffin.

"Jason told his father he was going to marry Maureen. He wouldn't be taking the football scholarship. Fitzpatrick pretended to understand, but he was furious. He was running out of time. He felt he had no choice but to act. His dreams would be over if Jason stayed around because of her. After dinner Jason went to his room to do homework. He left his phone on the kitchen table. Brian looked up Maureen's number and called her.

"He says it was an accident. But I think we can get him for premeditated murder. He told Maureen he wanted to make her an offer. Said he'd like to take her for a coffee and talk about it. She waited for him outside Stephanie Reynolds's house. Brian picked her up and drove her to a quiet spot near the Picton airfield. He offered her money to tell Jason it was over. She was to quit school and leave town for a year. Twenty thousand dollars if she'd have an abortion. Ten thousand if not. He thought Jason would come to his senses if Maureen left him." He sipped at his coffee.

"I assume Maureen said no."

"She told Brian she was in love with Jason. They were planning a life together. They and their child. He couldn't bear to think that his son was throwing his life away for her.

"She got out of the car, said she was feeling sick. She turned her back on him. He reached out and grabbed her scarf and twisted. Next thing he knew, she was dead."

I left out a long puff of air.

"He says he wanted to take her to the hospital. But he realized he'd be charged with killing her."

"No kidding."

"No kidding. So he left her by the side of the road. He wanted it to look like she'd been out for a walk and got picked up by some guy. Anyone going for a walk that night would have dressed very warmly, but Maureen wasn't wearing her gloves. He tried to make it look like a rape and started taking her pants off. A car came along and frightened him off."

"No," I said. "He wasn't trying to make it look like rape. More like a casual screw in the backseat of a car. One last chance to make Jason believe Maureen was a slut."

"You're probably right about that." He drank his coffee and took a bite out of an apple Danish.

"What's so sad," I said, "is that Brian Fitzpatrick was right all along."

"What do you mean?"

"Jason wanted to study for a law degree. He'd come home after class to a screaming baby. And its sixteen-year-old mother.

Tired and lonely. Angry because she wasn't having fun like other girls her age."

"What do you think they should have done?"

I shook my head. "Jason and Maureen had nothing but bad choices. It's a tragedy all around."

I got up and went to stand at the window. The roofs of the houses were piled with snow. Smoke rose from chimneys. The snowplow pushed its way up the street. I heard a siren getting closer. An OPP cruiser sped by. Its lights were flashing.

I went back to the table and finished my muffin.

VICKI DELANY is one of Canada's most prolific and varied crime writers. Her work includes stand-alone novels of psychological suspense, the Smith & Winters series and the Klondike Mystery series. Vicki enjoys the rural life in bucolic Prince Edward County, Ontario, where she grows vegetables, shovels snow and rarely wears a watch. For more information, visit www.vickidelany.com.

 **RAPID READS**

The following is an excerpt from
Orchestrated Murder, an exciting
Rapid Reads novel by Rick Blechta.

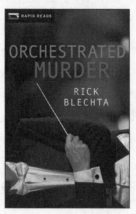

978-1-55469-885-1 $9.95 pb

Something is terribly wrong at Symphony Hall. Luigi
Spadafini, the symphony's star conductor, has been
murdered. With the mayor and several big shots from
the symphony's board of directors demanding a speedy
resolution of the crisis, Detective Lieutenant Pratt faces
a seemingly endless list of suspects with good reasons
to want the egotistical, philandering Spadafini dead.
But surely they didn't all kill him! Or did they?

CHAPTER ONE

Pratt felt like pounding his head on his desk. Why couldn't McDonnell just leave him alone today?

He felt every one of his fifty-four years as he walked past all the empty desks to the office of the man who ran the Homicide Division. His desk was as far away from the office as he could get it.

"What can I do for you?" Pratt asked.

Captain McDonnell looked up from the papers on his desk. "There's a problem at Symphony Hall. A big problem."

"What?"

"I've just had a call from upstairs. Appears someone's murdered the damn conductor."

"Luigi Spadafini?"

"Yes—if he's the conductor. I thought it would be right up your alley. You like this kind of music so much."

"Thanks," Pratt answered glumly.

What he wanted at the moment was a good nap, not another job. The previous night he'd been wrapping up a tricky case and got exactly three hours' sleep on a sofa in an empty office he'd found. He had the stiff neck to prove it too.

"The chief wants you to tread lightly. That's the other reason I'm sending you. You know how to act around the symphony set."

"Anything else?"

McDonnell shook his head. "Nope. Just hustle down there. Once the press gets hold of the news, all hell's going to break loose."

As Pratt turned to go, his boss added, "Take Ellis with you. Show him the ropes. This promises to be a little out of the ordinary."

Just great. Saddled with the greenest member of the squad. Pratt didn't even know the kid's first name and didn't care to. Hopefully the young pup wouldn't screw anything up.

As he went back to his desk, the captain called, "Good job last night, Pratt. You did us proud."

Pratt bit his tongue. Then why not let someone else handle this job and let him go home?

Pratt let Ellis drive across town to the city's latest municipal wonder. Built four years earlier to a lot of taxpayer squawking, Symphony Hall was beautiful outside but cold and sterile. Inside, though, it was all wood, and the sound quality was lovely. He'd heard Beethoven's Fifth Symphony there the previous month, and it had been a concert he'd remember for a long time. Spadafini had been very impressive.

Now Pratt's head felt as if it was stuffed with sawdust. Great way to begin an investigation.

Ellis was a good-looking lad. Tall and still lanky, a lot like Pratt when he'd been that age. Thirty years later, he'd lost most of his hair and put on a good fifty pounds. At least he didn't need glasses—yet.

Making conversation, he asked, "How long have you been in Homicide?

"Two weeks, sir," Ellis answered.

"Seen any action yet?"

"Only that domestic murder last Friday. Terrible situation. Mostly I've been pushing papers."

"So I heard."

"I wanted to say that it's an honor to be working with you."

"I don't need buttering up, Ellis. You're here to make my life easier. Keep your eyes and ears open and try to stay out of my way."

"My pleasure, sir."

"And another thing: stop calling me 'sir.' Pratt will do."

The coast was still clear as they pulled up at the backstage entrance. Surprisingly, the media hadn't arrived yet. A beat cop Pratt recognized was standing next to the door, looking bored.

"Glad to have you aboard, sir," he said. "It's a madhouse in there, I hear."

"It's going to be a madhouse out here too. Don't let anyone in, and don't tell them anything."

"Right."

Later on Pratt was sorry that he had just rushed by. He might have retired on the spot if he'd known about the unholy mess he was walking into.

At the vacant security desk just inside, a sergeant Pratt knew was waiting.

Next to him stood a man wearing a suit and tie, even though it was Saturday morning. He looked to be in his late thirties, medium height, slightly overweight.

"Glad they sent you, Pratt," the sergeant said as they shook hands. "This is Michael Browne. He's the symphony's manager. He's the one who called the murder in."

Pratt knew Browne had to be competent to have this sort of job. At the moment, he looked pretty rattled and on edge.

More handshaking as Pratt introduced Ellis.

"The situation is a real mess," the sergeant added.

"Blood?" the detective asked. He hated the bloody ones.

"No, no. It's the suspect list."

"What about it?"

"The entire orchestra has confessed."

blurted out :—
basked :—
sputtered :—

Titles in the Series

 **RAPID READS**